Embracing Resilience" A Story of Love Beyond Illness

BY
DERICK CHIBILu
&
ROBERT CHIBILU

Published by Books By Derick Chibilu, 2024.

Table of Contents

"Embracing Resilience"

A Story of Love Beyond Illness

BY

DERICK CHIBILU

&

ROBERT CHIBILU

****

Copyright © 2024 Books by Derick Chibilu

Published by Books by Derick Chibilu
12000 Sawmill Rd Suite 2213, The Woodlands,
TX, United States, Texas
Website: www.booksbyderikchibilu.com[1]
Email: Thecblogger4@gmail.com
Contact Number: +1 346-328-1110
Publication Date: 04/18/2024
Cover design by Dacisco Video and Media Production Team

Publisher's Note:

"Welcome to " Embracing Resilience" A Story of Love Beyond Illness.

For permission requests, please contact the publisher at the address provided above or you can visit our

www.booksbyderickchibilu.com.[2]

---

1. http://www.booksbyderikchibilu.com

2. http://www.booksbyderickchibilu.com.

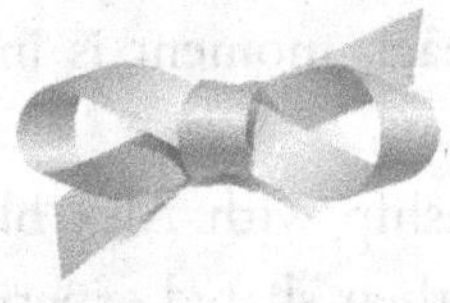

Book Description:

"Embracing Resilience" is a poignant narrative that delves deep into the life of Sarah, a courageous young woman grappling with the daily challenges of sickle cell disease. Raised in a supportive yet protective family environment, Sarah's journey unfolds against the backdrop of a vibrant community where she navigates the complexities of her condition with unwavering determination.

Born into a family that cherishes love and unity, Sarah's upbringing instilled in her the values of resilience and perseverance. However, her chronic illness casts a shadow over her aspirations, causing her to grapple with feelings of inadequacy and self-doubt, particularly in the realm of romantic relationships.

Chapter by chapter, readers are immersed in Sarah's world as she confronts her deepest fears and insecurities. From the daunting prospect of venturing into the realm of dating to the heart-wrenching moments of vulnerability during her first physical date with Alex, Sarah's journey is a testament to the human spirit's capacity to endure and triumph over adversity.

Set against the backdrop of a bustling urban landscape, the story captures the essence of Sarah's surroundings, from the quaint coffee shops where she meets Alex to the tranquil parks where they share intimate conversations. Through vivid descriptions and evocative imagery, readers are transported into

Sarah's world, where each moment is imbued with hope and possibility.

As Sarah's relationship with Alex blossoms, she discovers newfound strength in their shared experiences and unwavering support. Together, they navigate the complexities of her illness with grace and resilience, forging a bond that transcends the confines of physical limitations.

But amidst the joys of newfound love, Sarah must also confront personal challenges and familial expectations that threaten to derail her journey. Through poignant interactions with her family and friends, Sarah grapples with the fear of disappointing her loved ones and the pressure to conform to societal norms.

Yet, it is through these trials and tribulations that Sarah discovers the true meaning of resilience and self-acceptance. With each obstacle she overcomes, Sarah emerges stronger and more determined to embrace life's uncertainties with unwavering courage.

"Embracing Resilience" is not merely a tale of love and romance; it is a powerful testament to the indomitable spirit of the human heart and the transformative power of self-belief. As readers journey alongside Sarah, they are reminded that love knows no boundaries and that true happiness lies in embracing one's authentic self, flaws and all.

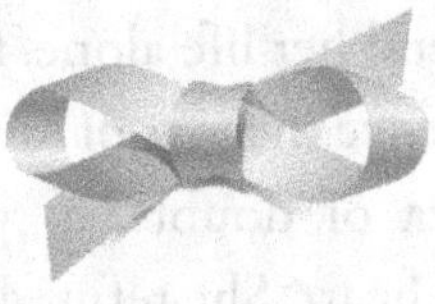

Chapter 1: The Fear of Dating

Sarah sat alone in her room, her fingers nervously tapping against the keyboard as she stared at the screen. She had been contemplating this moment for weeks, grappling with a mixture of excitement and trepidation. At eighteen years old, she knew she was finally of age to start dating, yet the thought of putting herself out there filled her with an overwhelming sense of dread.

As she glanced at the mirror across the room, Sarah's gaze lingered on the faint scars that marred her skin, a constant reminder of the battles she had fought against her relentless adversary: sickle cell disease. It was a condition that had shaped every aspect of her life, from the mundane routines of daily medication to the debilitating pain crises that often left her bedridden for days on end.

But it wasn't just the physical toll of her illness that weighed heavily on Sarah's mind; it was the emotional scars that ran much deeper. She had grown accustomed to the sympathetic glances and well-meaning inquiries from friends and family, but when it came to matters of the heart, Sarah couldn't shake the nagging fear that her condition would be a barrier to finding love.

With a sigh, Sarah pushed aside her doubts and clicked on the dating app she had downloaded weeks ago. As she scrolled through the profiles, a wave of anxiety washed over her. What if no one wanted to date someone with a chronic illness? What if she was destined to spend her life alone, forever on the sidelines watching others experience the joys of love and companionship?

But amidst the sea of doubts, a spark of determination flickered within Sarah's heart. She refused to let her illness define her or dictate her worth. She was more than just a medical diagnosis; she was a young woman with dreams and desires, longing for connection and intimacy like anyone else.

With a newfound resolve, Sarah began to craft her profile, choosing her words carefully to convey both her vulnerability and her strength. She didn't hide the fact that she had sickle cell disease; instead, she embraced it as a part of who she was, a testament to her resilience in the face of adversity.

As she uploaded a few photos and hit the "submit" button, Sarah felt a surge of anticipation mixed with apprehension. She didn't know what the future held or whether anyone would be interested in getting to know her beyond her illness, but one thing was certain: she was ready to face her fears and embark on this journey of self-discovery.

Little did Sarah know that her decision to embrace vulnerability would set the stage for a remarkable journey of love, resilience, and self-discovery that would captivate readers around the world.

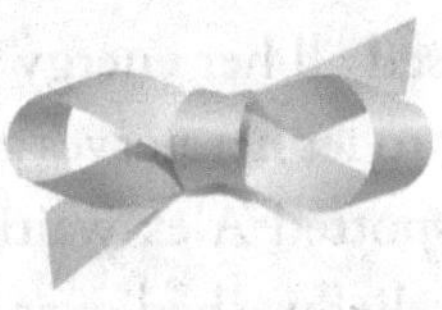

Chapter 2: The First Physical Date

The anticipation hung heavy in the air as Sarah stood in front of her closet, pondering over what to wear for her first physical date with Alex. It had been weeks since they first connected online, and their virtual conversations had blossomed into a deep and meaningful connection. Yet, despite the comfort of their digital interactions, Sarah couldn't shake the nervous flutter in her stomach as she prepared to meet Alex face-to-face for the first time.

As she carefully selected an outfit that struck the perfect balance between casual and chic, Sarah's mind raced with a whirlwind of emotions. She couldn't help but wonder how Alex would react upon seeing her in person, her not-too-shaped physical body a stark contrast to the polished images she had carefully curated on her profile. Would he still find her attractive, flaws and all? Or would he be repelled by the reality of her illness?

With a deep breath, Sarah silenced the doubts that threatened to consume her and reminded herself of the courage it had taken to put herself out there in the first place. She refused to let her insecurities overshadow the possibility of finding love, even if it meant facing rejection head-on.

As she stepped out of her apartment and made her way to the designated meeting spot, Sarah's heart raced with a potent mix of excitement and anxiety. The bustling city streets seemed to blur into a haze as she focused all her energy on maintaining a calm façade, determined not to let her nerves get the best of her.

When she finally spotted Alex waiting for her outside the coffee shop, a wave of relief washed over her. He smiled warmly as their eyes met, and Sarah felt a surge of gratitude for his reassuring presence. For a fleeting moment, all her fears melted away as she immersed herself in the warmth of his gaze.

As they exchanged pleasantries and settled into a cozy corner of the café, Sarah couldn't help but marvel at the ease with which they slipped into conversation. Their virtual rapport translated seamlessly into the real world, and Sarah found herself drawn to Alex's genuine curiosity and kindness.

But as the conversation flowed effortlessly between them, Sarah couldn't shake the gnawing uncertainty that lingered at the back of her mind. She knew that she couldn't keep her illness hidden forever, yet she feared that disclosing the truth would shatter the fragile connection they had forged.

As the afternoon stretched into evening, Sarah grappled with the decision weighing heavily on her shoulders. Should she muster the courage to reveal her condition to Alex, risking rejection and judgment? Or should she continue to conceal the truth, hiding behind a façade of normalcy?

Little did Sarah know that the choice she made in that pivotal moment would set the stage for a journey of love, resilience, and self-discovery that would defy all odds and inspire readers around the world.

Chapter 3: Overcoming Fears

As Sarah sat across from Alex in the cozy corner of the café, her heart raced with a tumultuous mix of emotions. The warmth of his smile offered her a glimmer of reassurance, yet the weight of her secret threatened to suffocate her. She knew that she couldn't keep the truth hidden any longer; the time had come to confront her fears and lay bare her vulnerability.

Summoning every ounce of courage within her, Sarah took a deep breath and mustered the strength to speak. With trembling hands and a voice laced with uncertainty, she began to share her truth with Alex, her words tumbling out in a torrent of raw honesty.

"I need to tell you something," Sarah began, her gaze fixed on the table as she struggled to find the right words. "I have sickle cell disease."

As the words hung in the air between them, Sarah braced herself for Alex's reaction. Would he recoil in horror at the revelation of her illness? Would he see her as damaged goods, unworthy of love and companionship? The seconds stretched into an eternity as Sarah waited with bated breath for his response.

To her astonishment, Alex's reaction was not one of revulsion or pity, but rather one of empathy and understanding. He reached across the table and gently took Sarah's hand in his own, his touch a soothing balm to her frayed nerves.

"Thank you for trusting me enough to share that with me," Alex said softly, his eyes filled with warmth and compassion. "I admire your strength and resilience in the face of such challenges."

In that moment, Sarah felt a weight lift off her shoulders as the walls she had built around her heart began to crumble. For the first time in her life, she allowed herself to believe that she was worthy of love, not in spite of her illness, but because of it.

As they continued to talk, Sarah and Alex delved deeper into their shared experiences, forging a bond that transcended the confines of their physical surroundings. With each passing moment, Sarah felt her fears and insecurities melt away as she basked in the warmth of Alex's acceptance and understanding.

Through her courageous act of vulnerability, Sarah had not only overcome her fears but had also discovered the true meaning of resilience and self-esteem. She realized that her illness did not define her; rather, it was a testament to her strength and tenacity in the face of adversity.

As they left the café hand in hand, Sarah knew that she was embarking on a journey unlike any she had ever known. With Alex by her side, she felt empowered to face whatever challenges lay ahead, knowing that their love would be the guiding light that illuminated their path.

Little did Sarah know that her act of bravery would set the stage for a love story that would captivate readers around the world, inspiring them to embrace their own vulnerabilities and overcome their deepest fears.

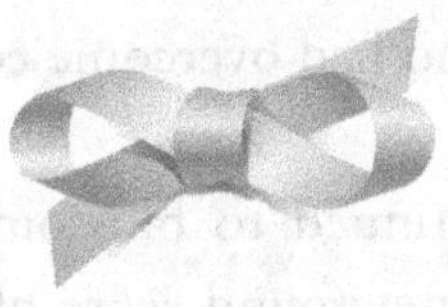

Chapter 4: Falling in Love

As Sarah and Alex's relationship blossomed, so too did their love for each other. With each passing day, they discovered new depths to their connection, weaving a tapestry of shared experiences and cherished memories that bound them together inextricably.

Their dates became adventures, as they explored the city hand in hand, laughing and talking as if they had known each other for a lifetime. From picnics in the park to late-night strolls beneath the stars, Sarah and Alex found solace and joy in each other's company, their laughter echoing through the night like a melody of hope and possibility.

But amidst the bliss of newfound love, Sarah couldn't shake the nagging doubt that lingered at the back of her mind. She knew that her illness would inevitably pose challenges to their relationship, and she feared that Alex would grow weary of bearing the burden of her care.

Yet, as she voiced her concerns to Alex one evening, his response filled her heart with a profound sense of reassurance. "I love you for who you are, Sarah," he said, his voice unwavering with conviction. "Your illness is just a part of you, and it doesn't change how I feel about you."

In that moment, Sarah felt a wave of gratitude wash over her as she realized the depth of Alex's love and devotion. He saw her not as a patient burdened by sickness, but as a resilient and courageous woman who had overcome countless obstacles with grace and dignity.

As their love continued to blossom, Sarah found herself embracing life with a newfound sense of purpose and passion. She no longer saw her illness as a barrier to happiness, but rather as a catalyst for growth and self-discovery.

Together, Sarah and Alex navigated the ups and downs of life with unwavering courage and resilience. They faced each challenge head-on, knowing that their love was stronger than any obstacle that stood in their way.

Through their journey of falling in love, Sarah and Alex became living testaments to the transformative power of resilience, love, and self-esteem. Their story inspired countless others to embrace their own vulnerabilities and pursue love with unwavering courage and conviction.

As they stood hand in hand, gazing into each other's eyes, Sarah knew that their love was not just a fleeting moment in time, but a timeless testament to the enduring power of the human spirit. And with Alex by her side, she knew that together, they could conquer anything that life threw their way.

Chapter 5: Discovering Strength

In the midst of Sarah's journey with Alex, she found herself confronting moments of adversity that tested her resilience and inner strength. It was during these challenging times that she discovered the depths of her own courage and determination, proving to herself and the world that she was more than just her illness.

One such moment came when Sarah experienced a particularly severe pain crisis, leaving her bedridden and wracked with agony. As she lay in the darkness of her room, her body consumed by pain, Sarah felt a wave of despair wash over her. In that moment of vulnerability, she questioned whether she had the strength to endure the relentless onslaught of her illness.

But as she reached out to Alex for support, she was met with an unwavering pillar of strength and love. He remained by her side through the long hours of the night, offering comfort and reassurance in the face of her suffering. His presence became a source of solace amidst the storm, reminding Sarah that she was not alone in her struggles.

As the pain gradually subsided and Sarah emerged from the depths of her despair, she felt a newfound sense of resilience stirring within her. She realized that her illness did not define her; rather, it was a testament to her strength and tenacity in the face of adversity.

Through her journey of discovering strength, Sarah learned to embrace her vulnerabilities and channel them into sources of power and resilience. She no longer saw her illness as a weakness, but rather as a badge of honor, symbolizing the battles she had fought and the victories she had won.

With each passing day, Sarah's self-esteem grew stronger, fueled by the unwavering love and support of Alex and the knowledge that she possessed the inner strength to overcome any obstacle that stood in her way.

As she reflected on her journey, Sarah realized that true strength was not measured by the absence of adversity, but rather by the courage to face it head-on and emerge stronger on the other side. And with Alex by her side, she knew that together, they could weather any storm that life threw their way.

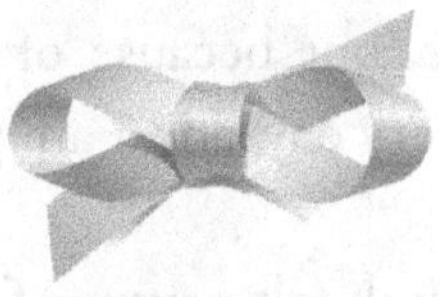

Chapter 6: Facing Insecurities

Despite the blossoming love between Sarah and Alex, insecurities continued to linger beneath the surface, threatening to undermine their happiness and stability. For Sarah, the fear of being judged and rejected because of her illness weighed heavily on her mind, casting a shadow over even the brightest moments of their relationship.

As they embarked on new adventures and shared intimate moments together, Sarah couldn't help but feel a pang of insecurity gnawing at her heart. She worried that Alex would grow tired of constantly accommodating her needs or that he would come to resent her for the limitations imposed by her illness.

These insecurities manifested themselves in subtle ways, causing Sarah to withdraw emotionally at times or to second-guess Alex's affections. She found herself caught in a vicious cycle of self-doubt, unable to shake the lingering fear that she was unworthy of love and belonging.

But as Sarah confided her fears to Alex one evening, she was met with a response that took her breath away. Instead of dismissing her concerns or brushing them aside, Alex listened with empathy and compassion, validating her feelings, and offering unwavering support.

"You are more than your illness, Sarah," Alex reassured her, his voice filled with sincerity. "I love you for who you are, not in spite of your illness, but because of it. Your strength and resilience inspire me every day, and I am grateful to have you in my life."

In that moment, Sarah felt a wave of relief wash over her as the walls of insecurity began to crumble around her. She realized that she didn't have to face her fears alone, that she had someone by her side who saw her for the remarkable woman she was, flaws and all.

Through their honest and open communication, Sarah and Alex confronted their insecurities head-on, forging a deeper bond rooted in trust and acceptance. They learned to lean on each other for support, to celebrate each other's victories, and to navigate the challenges of Sarah's illness with grace and resilience.

As Sarah faced her insecurities with courage and vulnerability, she discovered a newfound sense of self-esteem and self-worth. She no longer defined herself by her limitations but rather by the strength and resilience that had carried her through life's greatest trials.

Through their journey of facing insecurities, Sarah and Alex became living testaments to the transformative power of love, resilience, and self-acceptance. Their story inspired countless others to confront their own insecurities with courage and compassion, knowing that true happiness lay in embracing their authentic selves, flaws and all.

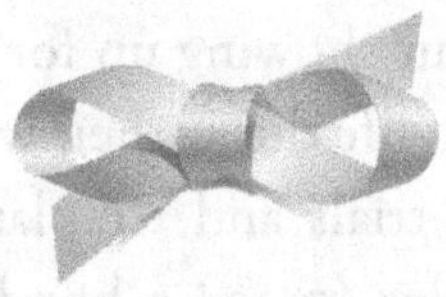

Chapter 7: Building Trust

Trust is the cornerstone of any relationship, and for Sarah and Alex, it was the foundation upon which their love story was built. As they navigated the complexities of Sarah's illness and the challenges it presented, they discovered that trust was not just about believing in each other, but also in themselves.

For Sarah, trusting Alex meant relinquishing control and allowing herself to be vulnerable, even when the fear of rejection threatened to consume her. It meant confiding her deepest fears and insecurities, knowing that Alex would hold her heart with gentleness and care.

As they embarked on this journey together, Sarah found herself grappling with moments of doubt and uncertainty. Would Alex stand by her side when the going got tough? Would he honor his promises and remain faithful to their love, even in the face of adversity?

But with each passing day, Sarah's trust in Alex grew stronger, nurtured by the unwavering support and unwavering devotion he showered upon her. He showed up for her in ways she never thought possible, offering a shoulder to lean on and a hand to hold during her darkest moments.

Through their shared experiences and intimate conversations, Sarah and Alex learned to communicate openly and honestly, laying bare their hopes, dreams, and fears without reservation. They discovered that trust was not just about words, but about actions, about showing up for each other day in and day out, no matter what life threw their way.

As they faced the trials and tribulations of Sarah's illness together, Sarah and Alex forged a bond that transcended the physical realm, a bond built on trust, respect, and unwavering love. They learned to lean on each other for support, to celebrate each other's victories, and to weather life's storms with courage and resilience.

Through their journey of building trust, Sarah and Alex became living testaments to the transformative power of love and resilience. Their story inspired countless others to believe in the power of trust, knowing that with trust as their guiding light, they could overcome any obstacle and conquer any challenge that stood in their way.

As Sarah and Alex stood hand in hand, gazing into each other's eyes, they knew that their love was built to last, grounded in the unshakeable foundation of trust. And with trust as their compass, they embarked on the next chapter of their journey together, knowing that whatever the future held, they would face it hand in hand, with hearts full of love and trust.

Chapter 8: Sharing Vulnerabilities

In the sanctuary of their love, Sarah and Alex discovered the transformative power of sharing vulnerabilities. As they peeled back the layers of their hearts and laid bare their deepest fears and insecurities, they forged a bond that transcended the confines of their physical existence.

For Sarah, sharing her vulnerabilities meant confronting the lingering doubts and insecurities that had plagued her for so long. It meant allowing herself to be seen in her most raw and unfiltered state, trusting that Alex would accept her flaws and imperfections with open arms.

As they sat together in the quiet intimacy of their shared space, Sarah found the courage to share the innermost recesses of her soul with Alex. She spoke of the moments of despair and doubt that had clouded her mind, of the fear of being judged and rejected because of her illness.

To her astonishment, Alex listened with empathy and understanding, his love shining like a beacon of hope amidst the darkness of her fears. He held her close, offering comfort and reassurance as she laid bare the scars of her past and the vulnerabilities of her heart.

Through their shared vulnerability, Sarah and Alex discovered a deeper connection that transcended the boundaries of words. They learned to hold space for each other's pain and insecurities, offering solace and support in times of need.

As they bared their souls to each other, Sarah and Alex realized that vulnerability was not a sign of weakness, but rather a testament to the strength and courage it took to show up authentically in the world. They embraced their vulnerabilities as sources of power and resilience, knowing that it was through their shared vulnerability that they found strength in each other's arms.

Through their journey of sharing vulnerabilities, Sarah and Alex became living testaments to the transformative power of love and resilience. Their story inspired countless others to embrace their own vulnerabilities, knowing that true intimacy and connection could only be found through the courage to be vulnerable.

As Sarah and Alex held each other close, they knew that their love was built on a foundation of shared vulnerability, a foundation strong enough to weather any storm that life threw their way. And with hearts full of love and gratitude, they embraced the journey that lay ahead, knowing that together, they could conquer anything.

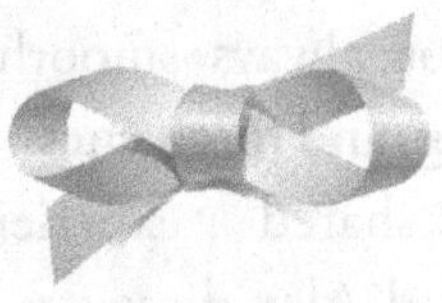

Chapter 9: Weathering Storms Together

As Sarah and Alex's love story unfolded, they found themselves facing unexpected storms that tested the strength of their bond. From sudden flare-ups of Sarah's illness to unforeseen challenges in their personal and professional lives, they learned that true resilience was not about avoiding the storms, but about weathering them together.

One such storm came when Sarah experienced a severe pain crisis that landed her in the hospital for days on end. As she lay in the sterile confines of her hospital room, her body racked with agony, Sarah felt a sense of helplessness wash over her. But amidst the darkness of her pain, she found solace in the unwavering presence of Alex by her side.

Throughout her hospital stay, Alex remained her steadfast companion, offering comfort and support in the face of her suffering. He held her hand through the long nights, whispering words of encouragement and love as they weathered the storm together.

But it wasn't just the physical storms that Sarah and Alex faced; they also encountered challenges in their relationship that tested the strength of their love. From misunderstandings and disagreements to moments of doubt and insecurity, they learned that true love was not always smooth sailing but required patience, understanding, and forgiveness.

Through their shared experiences and intimate conversations, Sarah and Alex discovered the true meaning of resilience. They learned to lean on each other for support, to draw strength from their love, and to face life's challenges with courage and grace.

As they weathered the storms together, Sarah and Alex grew closer, their bond forged in the fires of adversity. They realized that it was during the darkest moments that their love shone brightest, illuminating the path forward with hope and possibility.

Through their journey of weathering storms together, Sarah and Alex became living testaments to the transformative power of love and resilience. Their story inspired countless others to embrace the storms of life with courage and determination, knowing that with love as their anchor, they could overcome any obstacle that stood in their way.

As Sarah and Alex emerged from the storms stronger and more united than ever, they knew that their love was built to withstand the test of time. And with hearts full of gratitude and love, they embraced the journey that lay ahead, knowing that together, they could conquer anything that life threw their way.

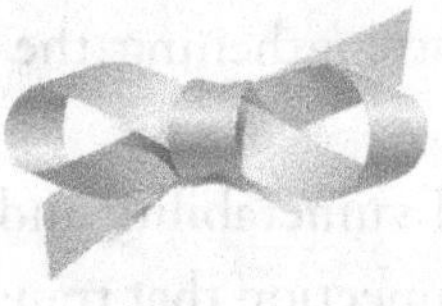

Chapter 10: A Heartfelt Confession

In the quiet solitude of a moonlit evening, Sarah found herself grappling with a truth that had long been buried deep within her heart. As she sat across from Alex, her fingers nervously entwined, she knew that the time had come to lay bare her soul and reveal the depths of her love.

With a trembling voice and a heart heavy with emotion, Sarah began to speak, her words a heartfelt confession that echoed through the stillness of the night. She spoke of the fears and insecurities that had plagued her for so long, of the doubts that had threatened to tear her apart from the inside out.

But amidst the darkness of her confessions, Sarah's voice was tinged with a glimmer of hope, a beacon of light that illuminated the depths of her love for Alex. She spoke of the ways in which he had touched her soul, of the joy and warmth he had brought into her life, of the ways in which he had shown her that love was not just a fleeting emotion but a steadfast commitment to be there for each other through thick and thin.

As Alex listened to Sarah's confession, his heart swelled with love and gratitude. He had known from the moment they met that Sarah was someone special, someone who had the power to change his life in ways he had never imagined possible. But hearing her heartfelt words of love and devotion touched him in a way he could never have anticipated, reaffirming his own feelings for her and strengthening the bond that held them together.

In that moment of vulnerability and truth, Sarah and Alex discovered a deeper connection that transcended the boundaries of words. They realized that true love was not just about grand gestures or extravagant displays of affection, but about the quiet moments of intimacy and vulnerability shared between two souls who were destined to be together.

Through her heartfelt confession, Sarah found liberation from the shackles of her own insecurities, embracing the fullness of her love for Alex without reservation or fear. And as they held each other close beneath the starry sky, they knew that their love was a force to be reckoned with, a bond that could withstand the tests of time and the trials of life.

Their heartfelt confession became a beacon of hope for all who dared to believe in the transformative power of love and resilience. It inspired countless others to embrace their own vulnerabilities and share their deepest truths with the ones they held dear, knowing that true happiness lay in the courage to be authentic and vulnerable with those who mattered most.

As Sarah and Alex embraced each other beneath the canopy of stars, they knew that their love was a gift to be cherished, a treasure to be held close to their hearts for all eternity. And with hearts full of love and gratitude, they embarked on the next chapter of their journey together, knowing that whatever the future held, they would face it hand in hand, with hearts full of love and a steadfast commitment to each other's happiness and well-being.

Chapter 11: Acceptance and Understanding

In the intricate dance of love and life, Sarah and Alex found themselves navigating the delicate balance between acceptance and understanding. As they journeyed through the highs and lows of Sarah's illness, they discovered that true acceptance was not about erasing the challenges they faced but about embracing them with open hearts and minds.

For Sarah, acceptance meant coming to terms with the realities of her illness and learning to love herself unconditionally, flaws and all. It meant releasing the shame and self-judgment that had held her captive for so long and embracing the beauty of her own resilience and strength.

With Alex by her side, Sarah embarked on a journey of self-discovery and acceptance, learning to see herself through the lens of love and compassion. She realized that her illness was not a curse but a blessing in disguise, a testament to her unwavering courage and determination in the face of adversity.

As they walked hand in hand through the corridors of uncertainty, Sarah and Alex discovered the power of understanding in fostering a deeper connection and intimacy. They learned to communicate openly and honestly, sharing their hopes, dreams, and fears without reservation or judgment.

Through their shared experiences and intimate conversations, Sarah and Alex cultivated a profound sense of understanding and empathy for each other's struggles. They learned to hold space for each other's pain and insecurities, offering solace and support in times of need.

As they embraced acceptance and understanding, Sarah and Alex realized that true love was not about fixing each other's flaws but about embracing them as integral parts of who they were. They learned to celebrate their differences and to support each other's growth and evolution as individuals and as partners.

Their journey of acceptance and understanding became a beacon of hope for all who dared to believe in the transformative power of love and resilience. It inspired countless others to embrace their own vulnerabilities and imperfections, knowing that true happiness lay in the courage to be authentic and vulnerable with those who mattered most.

As Sarah and Alex stood side by side, gazing into each other's eyes with hearts full of love and gratitude, they knew that their love was a testament to the enduring power of acceptance and understanding. And with each step they took together, they embraced the beauty of their journey, knowing that with love as their guiding light, they could conquer anything that life threw their way.

Chapter 12: Navigating Relationship Challenges

In the intricate tapestry of love, Sarah and Alex encountered a myriad of relationship challenges that tested the strength of their bond and the depth of their commitment to each other. From communication breakdowns to disagreements and misunderstandings, they learned that navigating these challenges required patience, understanding, and unwavering resilience.

One of the greatest challenges they faced was learning to communicate effectively in the midst of Sarah's illness. There were moments when Sarah's pain and fatigue made it difficult for her to express herself clearly, leading to frustration and tension between them. But through patience and perseverance, they discovered new ways to connect and communicate, finding solace in the simple act of being present with each other.

Another challenge arose when Sarah's illness interfered with their plans and expectations, forcing them to adapt and adjust to unforeseen circumstances. There were times when they had to cancel dates or change their plans at the last minute, leaving them feeling disappointed and disheartened. But through resilience and flexibility, they learned to embrace the unpredictability of life and find joy in the moments they shared together, regardless of the circumstances.

Yet another challenge came in the form of external pressures and judgments from friends and family members who didn't understand the complexities of Sarah's illness. There were moments when they faced criticism and skepticism from those who questioned the validity of their relationship or doubted Sarah's ability to be a good partner. But through solidarity and unwavering support for each other, they stood strong in the face of adversity, refusing to let the opinions of others dictate the course of their love story.

Through their journey of navigating relationship challenges, Sarah and Alex discovered the true meaning of resilience and perseverance. They learned that love was not always easy or straightforward but required dedication, commitment, and a willingness to weather the storms together.

Their story of overcoming obstacles and triumphing over adversity became a beacon of hope for all who dared to believe in the transformative power of love and resilience. It inspired countless others to embrace the challenges of their own relationships with courage and determination, knowing that with love as their compass, they could navigate even the stormiest seas.

As Sarah and Alex stood hand in hand, facing the unknown future with hearts full of love and optimism, they knew that their journey was far from over. But with each challenge they overcame and each obstacle they conquered, they grew stronger and more united in their love, proving that with resilience, love, and unwavering commitment, anything was possible.

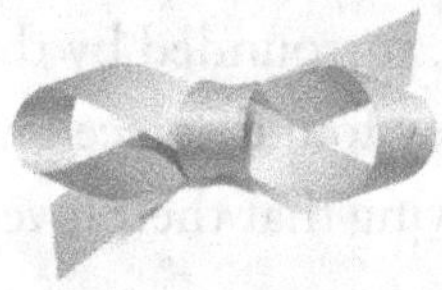

Chapter 13: Celebrating Small Victories

In the journey of life, Sarah and Alex learned to find joy and meaning in celebrating the small victories that dotted their path. From overcoming daily challenges to achieving personal milestones, they discovered that true happiness lay not in grand gestures or momentous achievements but in the simple joys of everyday life.

For Sarah, celebrating small victories meant finding gratitude and appreciation for the moments of joy and triumph that illuminated her journey with Alex. It meant rejoicing in the moments when her illness didn't hold her back, when she felt a surge of energy and vitality that allowed her to fully embrace life's possibilities.

One such small victory came when Sarah was able to go for a walk in the park with Alex without experiencing debilitating pain or fatigue. As they strolled hand in hand beneath the golden rays of the sun, Sarah felt a sense of freedom and liberation wash over her, knowing that she was no longer defined by her illness but by the strength and resilience that had carried her through life's greatest challenges.

Another small victory came when Sarah and Alex shared a quiet evening at home, cooking dinner together and laughing as they clumsily attempted to follow a new recipe. In the warmth of their shared kitchen, surrounded by the comforting aroma of home-cooked food, they found solace and joy in the simple act of being together, knowing that their love was the greatest gift of all.

Yet another small victory came when Sarah received a heartfelt letter from a friend expressing gratitude for her support and encouragement during a difficult time. As she read the words of appreciation and love, Sarah felt a sense of fulfillment and purpose wash over her, knowing that she had made a positive impact on someone else's life through her kindness and compassion.

Through their journey of celebrating small victories, Sarah and Alex discovered the true meaning of resilience and gratitude. They learned to find joy in the little moments that brought light into their lives, knowing that true happiness was not found in the pursuit of perfection but in the acceptance of life's imperfections.

Their story of finding joy in the midst of adversity became a beacon of hope for all who dared to believe in the transformative power of love and resilience. It inspired countless others to embrace the small victories that adorned their own journey, knowing that true happiness lay in the ability to find beauty and meaning in the everyday moments of life.

As Sarah and Alex stood hand in hand, gazing into each other's eyes with hearts full of love and gratitude, they knew that their journey was far from over. But with each small victory they celebrated and each moment of joy they shared, they grew stronger and more resilient in their love, proving that with gratitude and resilience, anything was possible.

Chapter 14: Finding Joy in Everyday Moments

In the hustle and bustle of life, amidst the chaos and challenges, Sarah and Alex discovered the profound beauty of finding joy in everyday moments. They realized that true happiness was not found in grand gestures or extraordinary events, but in the simple, often overlooked moments that filled their lives with meaning and purpose.

For Sarah, finding joy in everyday moments meant taking pleasure in the small miracles that unfolded around her each day. It meant savoring the warmth of the morning sun on her face, the soothing sound of rain tapping against her window, and the sweet melody of birdsong in the early hours of dawn.

One of Sarah's favorite moments of joy came during quiet evenings spent curled up on the couch with Alex, lost in the pages of a good book or engrossed in a heartfelt conversation. In those precious moments of togetherness, surrounded by the warmth of their love, Sarah felt a sense of contentment and fulfillment that filled her heart with gratitude.

Another moment of joy came when Sarah stumbled upon an old photo album filled with cherished memories from her childhood. As she flipped through the pages, laughter and tears mingling on her cheeks, Sarah found solace and comfort in the nostalgia of days gone by, knowing that those precious moments would live on in her heart forever.

Yet another moment of joy came when Sarah received a surprise visit from a dear friend she hadn't seen in years. As they embraced each other with tears of joy streaming down their faces, Sarah felt a sense of connection and belonging that filled her soul with happiness and love.

Through their journey of finding joy in everyday moments, Sarah and Alex discovered that happiness was not a destination to be reached but a journey to be embraced. They learned to slow down and savor the simple pleasures of life, knowing that true joy could be found in the present moment, no matter how fleeting or ordinary it may seem.

Their story of finding joy in everyday moments became a source of inspiration for all who dared to believe in the transformative power of gratitude and mindfulness. It reminded countless others to pause and appreciate the beauty that surrounded them, knowing that true happiness lay in the ability to find joy in the here and now.

As Sarah and Alex stood hand in hand, gazing into each other's eyes with hearts full of love and gratitude, they knew that their journey was far from over. But with each moment of joy they embraced and each memory they cherished, they grew stronger and more resilient in their love, proving that with gratitude and mindfulness, anything was possible.

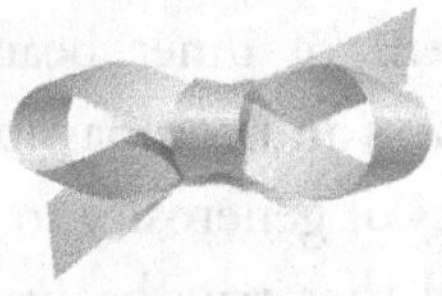

Chapter 15: Unveiling Inner Beauty

In the depths of their journey, Sarah and Alex embarked on a profound exploration of inner beauty, discovering that true radiance emanated from the depths of their souls rather than the surface of their skin. They realized that while society often placed emphasis on external appearances, it was the beauty of the heart and spirit that truly illuminated their lives.

For Sarah, unveiling inner beauty meant embracing her uniqueness and celebrating the qualities that made her who she was. It meant letting go of societal standards of beauty and embracing her scars, both physical and emotional, as badges of honor that told the story of her resilience and strength.

One of Sarah's most transformative moments came when she looked into the mirror and saw not her flaws but the beauty of her soul reflected back at her. In that moment of clarity, she realized that true beauty could not be measured by the size of her waist or the perfection of her features but by the kindness and compassion that radiated from her heart.

Another moment of revelation came when Sarah witnessed Alex's unwavering love and acceptance, despite her perceived imperfections. As he held her close and whispered words of affirmation and encouragement, Sarah felt a sense of liberation and empowerment wash over her, knowing that she was loved for who she was, unconditionally and without reservation.

Yet another moment of inner beauty came when Sarah witnessed acts of kindness and compassion in the world around her. From small gestures of generosity to acts of selflessness and sacrifice, Sarah realized that true beauty was not confined to physical appearances but shone brightly in the hearts of those who dared to love and care for others.

Through their journey of unveiling inner beauty, Sarah and Alex discovered that true radiance lay not in the pursuit of perfection but in the acceptance of their authentic selves. They learned to embrace their flaws and imperfections as sources of strength and resilience, knowing that true beauty was found in the courage to be vulnerable and authentic in a world that often valued conformity over individuality.

Their story of unveiling inner beauty became a beacon of hope for all who dared to believe in the transformative power of self-love and acceptance. It inspired countless others to embrace their own uniqueness and celebrate the beauty that resided within them, knowing that true happiness lay in the courage to be themselves, unapologetically and authentically.

As Sarah and Alex stood hand in hand, gazing into each other's eyes with hearts full of love and gratitude, they knew that their journey of unveiling inner beauty was far from over. But with each step they took towards self-discovery and self-acceptance, they grew stronger and more radiant in their love, proving that true beauty was not just skin deep but soul deep, and that it could light up the darkest corners of the world with its brilliance.

Chapter 16: Supportive Friends and Family

In the labyrinth of life, Sarah and Alex found solace and strength in the unwavering support of their friends and family. They discovered that amidst the trials and tribulations, having a supportive network of loved ones by their side could make all the difference in their journey towards healing, resilience, and love.

For Sarah, supportive friends and family became her pillars of strength during the darkest moments of her illness. They were the ones who stood by her side through the long nights of pain and uncertainty, offering comfort and encouragement when she needed it most.

One of Sarah's most poignant memories came when her best friend, Emily, dropped everything to accompany her to a doctor's appointment. As they sat together in the waiting room, Emily held Sarah's hand and offered words of reassurance, reminding her that she was not alone in her struggles.

Another moment of profound support came when Sarah's parents surprised her with a care package filled with homemade meals, comforting blankets, and heartfelt notes of love and encouragement. In that moment, Sarah felt a wave of gratitude wash over her, knowing that she was surrounded by a circle of love that would always be there to lift her up when she fell.

Yet another moment of support came when Alex's family welcomed Sarah into their home with open arms, embracing her as one of their own and showering her with love and acceptance. In their warm embrace, Sarah found a sense of belonging and security that filled her heart with warmth and gratitude.

Through their journey of navigating sickness, resilience, and love, Sarah and Alex realized that the love and support of their friends and family were invaluable treasures that sustained them through life's greatest challenges. They learned to lean on each other and on their loved ones for strength and encouragement, knowing that together, they could overcome any obstacle that stood in their way.

Their story of supportive friends and family became a testament to the power of love and connection in the face of adversity. It inspired countless others to cherish and nurture their relationships with loved ones, knowing that true happiness lay in the bonds of love and support that held them together.

As Sarah and Alex stood hand in hand, surrounded by their supportive network of friends and family, they knew that their journey was far from over. But with each hug, each word of encouragement, and each moment of shared laughter, they felt a sense of gratitude and love that filled their hearts to overflowing, knowing that they were truly blessed to have such incredible people by their side.

Chapter 17: Embracing Life's Imperfections

In the tapestry of life, Sarah and Alex learned to find beauty and meaning in life's imperfections, realizing that it was these very imperfections that made their journey unique and extraordinary. They discovered that true happiness and fulfillment could be found not in the pursuit of perfection, but in the acceptance and celebration of life's inherent flaws and complexities.

For Sarah, embracing life's imperfections meant letting go of the need to control every aspect of her illness and her life. It meant accepting that there would be good days and bad days, moments of triumph and moments of setback, and finding peace in the ebb and flow of life's ever-changing currents.

One of Sarah's most transformative moments came when she realized that her illness did not define her, but was simply a part of who she was. In that moment of acceptance, Sarah felt a weight lift off her shoulders, knowing that she was so much more than her sickness and that she was worthy of love and acceptance just as she was.

Another moment of embracing life's imperfections came when Sarah and Alex encountered challenges in their relationship that threatened to tear them apart. Instead of trying to fix every problem or smooth over every disagreement, they learned to embrace the messiness of love and relationships, knowing that true intimacy and connection could only be found in vulnerability and authenticity.

Yet another moment of embracing life's imperfections came when Sarah witnessed moments of raw beauty and grace in the midst of chaos and disorder. From the laughter of children playing in the streets to the vibrant colors of a sunset painting the sky, Sarah realized that true beauty could be found in the unlikeliest of places, if only one had the eyes to see it.

Through their journey of embracing life's imperfections, Sarah and Alex discovered that true happiness and fulfillment lay not in the pursuit of perfection, but in the acceptance and celebration of life's inherent messiness and complexity. They learned to embrace the highs and lows, the triumphs and setbacks, knowing that each moment, no matter how imperfect, was a precious gift to be cherished and savored.

Their story of embracing life's imperfections became a source of inspiration for all who dared to believe in the transformative power of acceptance and authenticity. It reminded countless others to let go of the need for control and perfection, and to embrace the beautiful messiness of life with open arms and open hearts.

As Sarah and Alex stood hand in hand, gazing into each other's eyes with hearts full of love and gratitude, they knew that their journey of embracing life's imperfections was far from over. But with each moment of acceptance and celebration, they grew stronger and more resilient in their love, proving that true happiness could be found in the imperfections of life, if only one had the courage to embrace them.

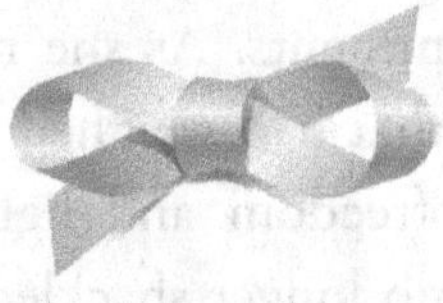

Chapter 18: Letting Go of Fear

In the journey of self-discovery and love, Sarah and Alex confronted their deepest fears and learned the transformative power of letting go. They realized that fear was often the greatest obstacle standing in the way of their happiness and fulfillment, and that true liberation could only be found in the courage to release their grip on the things that held them back.

For Sarah, letting go of fear meant confronting the fears that had long haunted her dreams and aspirations. It meant facing the uncertainty of her illness with grace and resilience, knowing that she was stronger and more capable than she had ever imagined.

One of Sarah's most pivotal moments came when she realized that her fear of rejection was holding her back from fully embracing love and intimacy. In that moment of clarity, Sarah made a conscious decision to let go of her fear and allow herself to be vulnerable, knowing that true connection could only be found in the absence of fear and inhibition.

Another moment of letting go of fear came when Sarah and Alex decided to take a leap of faith and pursue their dreams together. Despite the uncertainty and risks that lay ahead, they refused to let fear dictate their decisions, knowing that true fulfillment could only be found in the pursuit of their passions and desires.

Yet another moment of liberation came when Sarah witnessed the transformative power of forgiveness in letting go of past hurts and resentments. As she released the burden of anger and resentment that had weighed her down for so long, Sarah felt a sense of freedom and lightness wash over her, knowing that she was no longer shackled by the chains of fear and bitterness.

Through their journey of letting go of fear, Sarah and Alex discovered that true liberation could only be found in the absence of fear and inhibition. They learned to embrace the unknown with open hearts and minds, knowing that true growth and transformation could only be found on the other side of fear.

Their story of letting go of fear became a beacon of hope for all who dared to believe in the transformative power of courage and resilience. It inspired countless others to confront their deepest fears and insecurities, knowing that true happiness and fulfillment lay on the other side of fear.

As Sarah and Alex stood hand in hand, gazing into each other's eyes with hearts full of love and gratitude, they knew that their journey of letting go of fear was far from over. But with each step they took towards liberation and self-discovery, they grew stronger and more resilient in their love, proving that true happiness could only be found in the absence of fear and inhibition.

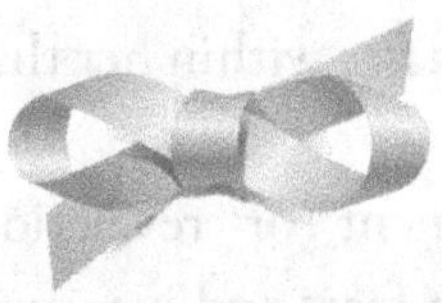

Chapter 19: A Journey of Self-Discovery

O very, unraveling the mysteries of their own hearts and minds as they navigated the twists and turns of love, resilience, and healing. They realized that true fulfillment and happiness could only be found by delving deep within themselves and uncovering the hidden truths that lay dormant within.

For Sarah, the journey of self-discovery began with a simple question: Who am I? In her quest for self-awareness and understanding, Sarah embarked on a journey of introspection and reflection, peeling back the layers of societal conditioning and expectations to reveal the essence of her true self.

One of Sarah's most transformative moments came when she embraced her vulnerabilities and imperfections as integral parts of her identity. In that moment of acceptance and self-love, Sarah discovered a newfound sense of freedom and authenticity that empowered her to live her life with courage and conviction.

Another moment of self-discovery came when Sarah uncovered her true passions and desires, following the whisperings of her heart to pursue her dreams with unwavering determination and purpose. In the pursuit of her passions, Sarah found a sense of purpose and fulfillment that breathed new life into her soul, igniting a fire within her that burned brightly with hope and possibility.

Yet another moment of revelation came when Sarah confronted her deepest fears and insecurities, shining a light on the shadows that lurked within and finding the strength and resilience to overcome them. In the face of adversity, Sarah discovered the depths of her own courage and resilience, emerging from the darkness stronger and more resilient than ever before.

Through their journey of self-discovery, Sarah and Alex learned to embrace the fullness of who they were, unapologetically and authentically. They realized that true happiness and fulfillment could only be found by living in alignment with their true selves, honoring their passions, and embracing their vulnerabilities with open hearts and minds.

Their story of self-discovery became a source of inspiration for all who dared to embark on the journey of self-awareness and understanding. It reminded countless others to listen to the whispers of their hearts, to embrace their vulnerabilities, and to live their lives with courage and conviction, knowing that true fulfillment and happiness lay in the depths of their own souls.

As Sarah and Alex stood hand in hand, gazing into each other's eyes with hearts full of love and gratitude, they knew that their journey of self-discovery was far from over. But with each step they took towards authenticity and self-acceptance, they grew stronger and more resilient in their love, proving that true happiness could only be found by embracing the fullness of who they were, flaws and all.

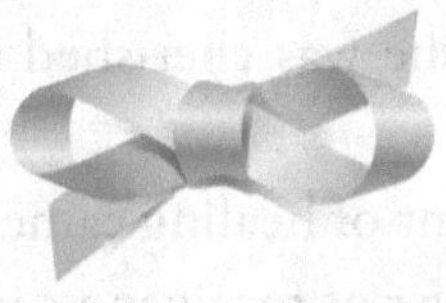

Chapter 20: Love's Healing Power

In the intricate tapestry of life, Sarah and Alex discovered the profound healing power of love, a force that transcended all boundaries and transformed their journey of sickness and resilience into a symphony of hope and renewal. They realized that love had the miraculous ability to mend broken hearts, soothe wounded souls, and illuminate even the darkest corners of their lives with its radiant light.

For Sarah, love became the balm that soothed the wounds of her illness and lifted her spirits during the darkest moments of despair. It was the unwavering support and unconditional acceptance of Alex that gave her the strength and courage to face each day with renewed hope and determination.

One of Sarah's most transformative moments came when she experienced the healing power of love in the embrace of her family and friends. Their love became a source of comfort and solace, wrapping her in a warm cocoon of support and understanding that eased her pain and lifted her spirits during the most challenging times.

Another moment of healing came when Sarah and Alex shared intimate moments of connection and vulnerability, allowing their love to flow freely between them like a healing balm that soothed the wounds of their past and revitalized their spirits for the journey ahead. In the sanctuary of their love, Sarah found a sense of peace and wholeness that she had never known before, knowing that she was cherished and adored just as she was.

Yet another moment of healing came when Sarah witnessed the transformative power of forgiveness in her relationship with herself and others. As she let go of past grievances and embraced forgiveness with an open heart, Sarah felt a weight lift off her shoulders, freeing her from the burdens of anger and resentment that had held her back for so long.

Through their journey of experiencing love's healing power, Sarah and Alex learned that true healing could only be found in the depths of their own hearts, where love resided as a constant and unwavering presence. They realized that love was not just an emotion, but a powerful force that had the ability to heal even the deepest wounds and restore wholeness to their lives.

Their story of love's healing power became a beacon of hope for all who dared to believe in the transformative power of love. It inspired countless others to open their hearts to love's healing embrace, knowing that true healing and renewal could only be found in the depths of love's boundless ocean.

As Sarah and Alex stood hand in hand, gazing into each other's eyes with hearts full of love and gratitude, they knew that their journey of healing and renewal was far from over. But with each moment of love and connection they shared, they grew stronger and more resilient in their love, proving that love was the greatest healer of all, capable of transforming even the darkest of nights into the brightest of dawns.

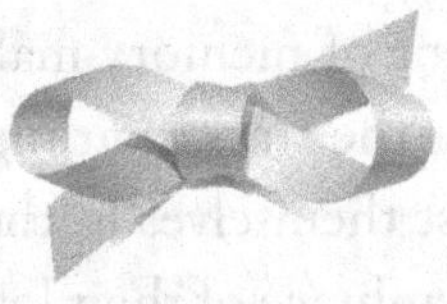

Chapter 21: Making Memories

In the tapestry of their lives, Sarah and Alex cherished the art of making memories, weaving together moments of joy, laughter, and love that would last a lifetime. They realized that amidst the trials and tribulations of their journey, it was the memories they created together that became the threads binding them closer, filling their hearts with warmth and gratitude.

For Sarah, making memories meant embracing every moment with open arms and an open heart, knowing that each experience, no matter how small or seemingly insignificant, held the potential to become a cherished memory that would be etched into the fabric of her life forever.

One of Sarah's most treasured memories came when she and Alex embarked on a spontaneous road trip, venturing into the unknown and embracing the adventure that awaited them around every corner. From winding country roads to bustling city streets, they explored the world together, creating memories that would last a lifetime.

Another moment of memory-making came when Sarah and Alex shared intimate dinners by candlelight, lost in conversation and laughter as they savored the simple pleasure of each other's company. In those moments of togetherness, surrounded by the warmth of their love, Sarah felt a sense of contentment and fulfillment that filled her heart with gratitude.

Yet another moment of memory-making came when Sarah and Alex danced under the stars, twirling and spinning in each other's arms as they lost themselves in the music and the magic of the moment. In the embrace of their love, Sarah felt as though time stood still, allowing them to savor the sweetness of the present moment with all its beauty and wonder.

Through their journey of making memories, Sarah and Alex learned to treasure each moment as a precious gift, knowing that life was made up of a series of moments that would soon become memories. They realized that true happiness could be found in the simple pleasures of life, in the laughter of loved ones, and in the warmth of shared experiences.

Their story of making memories became a source of inspiration for all who dared to embrace the beauty of the present moment and create lasting memories with the ones they loved. It reminded countless others to seize every opportunity for adventure, laughter, and love, knowing that true fulfillment could be found in the memories they created along the way.

As Sarah and Alex stood hand in hand, gazing into each other's eyes with hearts full of love and gratitude, they knew that their journey of making memories was far from over. But with each moment they shared, each memory they created, they grew stronger and more resilient in their love, proving that true happiness could be found in the beauty of life's fleeting moments, captured forever in the tapestry of their hearts.

Chapter 22: Planning for the Future

In the midst of their journey of love and resilience, Sarah and Alex found themselves looking towards the future with hope and anticipation, eager to build a life filled with love, purpose, and possibility. They realized that despite the challenges they had faced, the future held endless opportunities for growth, adventure, and happiness.

For Sarah, planning for the future meant envisioning a life filled with love, laughter, and fulfillment, despite the uncertainties that lay ahead. It meant setting goals and aspirations that reflected her deepest desires and passions, and taking concrete steps towards turning her dreams into reality.

One of Sarah's most transformative moments came when she and Alex sat down together to create a vision board, mapping out their dreams and aspirations for the future. From travel adventures to career goals, they visualized the life they wanted to create together, setting their intentions and aligning their actions with their dreams.

Another moment of future planning came when Sarah and Alex discussed their shared values and priorities, laying the foundation for a future built on a solid bedrock of love, trust, and mutual respect. In those conversations, they forged a deeper connection and understanding, knowing that they were on the same page when it came to their hopes and dreams for the future.

Yet another moment of anticipation came when Sarah and Alex made plans for their future home, envisioning a place filled with warmth, love, and laughter, where they could build a life together surrounded by the people and things they cherished most.

Through their journey of planning for the future, Sarah and Alex learned to embrace the unknown with open hearts and minds, knowing that the future held endless possibilities for growth and fulfillment. They realized that true happiness could be found not in the destination, but in the journey itself, and that every step they took towards their dreams brought them closer to the life they had always envisioned.

Their story of planning for the future became a source of inspiration for all who dared to dream big and pursue their passions with courage and conviction. It reminded countless others to set goals and aspirations that reflected their deepest desires, and to take bold action towards creating the life they truly wanted.

As Sarah and Alex stood hand in hand, gazing into each other's eyes with hearts full of love and anticipation, they knew that their journey of planning for the future was just beginning. But with each step they took towards their dreams, they grew stronger and more resilient in their love, proving that true happiness could be found in the pursuit of a life filled with purpose, passion, and possibility.

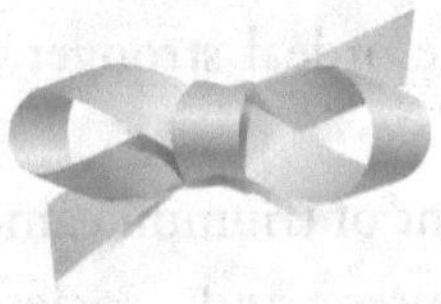

Chapter 23: A Leap of Faith

In the tapestry of their journey, Sarah and Alex encountered numerous obstacles that tested their resilience, challenged their love, and pushed them to their limits. Yet, through unwavering determination and the power of their love, they discovered that no obstacle was insurmountable when faced together.

For Sarah, overcoming obstacles together meant leaning on Alex for support during the darkest moments of her illness, knowing that his love and encouragement would light her way through the storm. It meant facing each challenge with courage and conviction, knowing that together they were stronger than any obstacle that stood in their path.

One of Sarah's most defining moments came when she faced a health crisis that threatened to derail her dreams and aspirations. In that moment of uncertainty and fear, Sarah turned to Alex for strength and support, finding solace in his unwavering belief in her ability to overcome any obstacle that came her way.

Another moment of overcoming obstacles together came when Sarah and Alex encountered challenges in their relationship that tested the very foundation of their love. Instead of allowing those challenges to tear them apart, they chose to confront them head-on, communicating openly and honestly, and emerging from the ordeal stronger and more united than ever before.

Yet another moment of triumph came when Sarah and Alex faced external pressures and societal expectations that threatened to undermine their happiness and fulfillment. In the face of adversity, they stood firm in their love and commitment to each other, refusing to let anyone or anything come between them and their shared dreams.

Through their journey of overcoming obstacles together, Sarah and Alex learned that true strength and resilience could only be found in the depths of their love and connection. They realized that every obstacle they faced was an opportunity for growth and transformation, and that together, they could conquer anything that stood in their way.

Their story of overcoming obstacles together became a source of inspiration for all who dared to believe in the power of love and resilience. It reminded countless others that no matter how daunting the challenges they faced, they were never alone as long as they had the love and support of those who stood by their side.

As Sarah and Alex stood hand in hand, gazing into each other's eyes with hearts full of love and gratitude, they knew that their journey of overcoming obstacles together was far from over. But with each challenge they faced, each obstacle they conquered, they grew stronger and more resilient in their love, proving that true happiness could be found in the strength of their bond and the power of their love to overcome any obstacle that stood in their way.

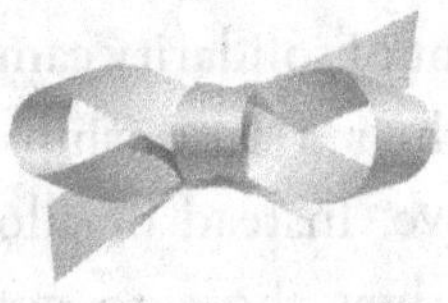

Chapter 24: Strength

As Sarah and Alex navigated the ebbs and flows of their journey, they discovered the profound strength that lay in their unity, a force that bound them together through the trials and triumphs of life. They realized that their love and resilience were amplified when they stood united, facing the challenges of sickness, adversity, and self-discovery as a cohesive team.

For Sarah, strength in unity meant finding solace in the unwavering support and understanding of Alex, knowing that together they could weather any storm that came their way. It meant standing shoulder to shoulder with Alex, facing their fears and uncertainties with courage and conviction, and emerging stronger and more resilient with each challenge they overcame.

One of Sarah's most empowering moments came when she and Alex faced a difficult decision that required them to lean on each other for support and guidance. In the face of uncertainty, they found strength in their unity, trusting in each other's judgment and standing firm in their shared values and priorities.

Another moment of unity came when Sarah and Alex confronted external pressures and societal expectations that threatened to divide them. Instead of allowing those pressures to tear them apart, they chose to stand united, reaffirming their commitment to each other and refusing to let anyone or anything come between them.

Yet another moment of solidarity came when Sarah and Alex faced challenges in their relationship that tested the very foundation of their love. Instead of allowing those challenges to drive them apart, they chose to confront them together, communicating openly and honestly, and emerging from the ordeal stronger and more connected than ever before.

Through their journey of strength in unity, Sarah and Alex learned that true resilience and love could only be found in the depths of their connection and commitment to each other. They realized that by standing united, they could overcome any obstacle that stood in their way, and emerge stronger and more united on the other side.

Their story of strength in unity became a beacon of hope for all who dared to believe in the transformative power of love and resilience. It reminded countless others that true strength could be found in the unity of hearts and minds, and that together, they could conquer even the greatest challenges that life threw their way.

As Sarah and Alex stood hand in hand, gazing into each other's eyes with hearts full of love and gratitude, they knew that their journey of strength in unity was far from over. But with each step they took together, each obstacle they overcame, they grew stronger and more resilient in their love, proving that true happiness could be found in the strength of their unity and the power of their love to overcome any obstacle that stood in their way.

Chapter 25: Forever and Always

Sarah and Alex stood hand in hand, surrounded by the warmth and beauty of their love, they knew that their journey had led them to this moment, a moment of profound connection and deep fulfillment. Through the trials and triumphs they had faced together, they had discovered the true meaning of love, resilience, and self-esteem, forging a bond that would last forever and always.

For Sarah, the journey had been one of self-discovery and transformation, a journey that had led her to embrace her true self and find strength in her vulnerabilities. Through the love and support of Alex, she had learned to see herself through the lens of unconditional love, recognizing her inherent worth and beauty as a child of God.

One of Sarah's most powerful realizations came when she understood that her sickness did not define her, but rather, it was a part of her journey that had shaped her into the person she had become. Through her resilience and determination, she had overcome the obstacles that had once seemed insurmountable, emerging stronger and more empowered than ever before.

Another moment of clarity came when Sarah embraced the teachings of Christ on love and forgiveness, recognizing that true happiness could only be found in loving unconditionally and forgiving freely. In the Sermon on the Mount, Christ had taught His disciples to love their enemies, bless those who cursed them, and pray for those who persecuted them, embodying the spirit of unconditional love and compassion that Sarah and Alex sought to emulate in their own lives.

Through their journey of love and resilience, Sarah and Alex had learned valuable lessons that they hoped to share with others. They had learned that true happiness could only be found in loving unconditionally, forgiving freely, and embracing the inherent worth and dignity of every human being.

As they reflected on their journey, Sarah and Alex felt a deep sense of gratitude for the love and support they had received along the way. They knew that their story was not just their own, but a testament to the power of love to transform lives and bring healing to the brokenhearted.

And so, as Sarah and Alex looked towards the future with hope and anticipation, they vowed to continue their journey of love and resilience, knowing that with faith and courage, they could overcome any obstacle that stood in their way. For they knew that with love as their guide, they could weather any storm and emerge stronger and more united on the other side.

As the final pages of their story came to a close, Sarah and Alex left behind a legacy of love and resilience that would inspire generations to come. Theirs was a story of hope, of faith, and of the transformative power of love to heal, to restore, and to renew.

Through Sarah and Alex's journey, we learn that true happiness and fulfillment come from embracing our true selves, loving unconditionally, and facing life's challenges with courage and resilience. Their story reminds us that we are worthy of love and acceptance just as we are, and that by loving others unconditionally, we can create a world filled with compassion, empathy, and understanding.

As readers, let us heed the call to love unconditionally, as Christ taught us in the Sermon on the Mount. Let us strive to be good ambassadors of the Gospel of Jesus Christ, embodying the spirit of love, forgiveness, and compassion in all that we do. For it is through our actions and our words that we can bring healing and hope to a world in need of love and grace. Let us commit to loving others as Christ loves us, forever and always.

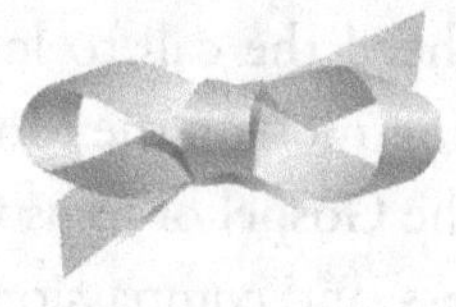

ABOUT THE AUTHOR

Derick Chibilu is an upcoming talented author and business professional based in Houston, Texas, where he resides with his beloved wife, Alice, and is known for his inspiring works. Derick holds an MBA from Capella University, a Bachelor of Business in Computer Information Systems from the University of Houston Downtown (UHD), and an Associate of Science in Business Administration from Delaware Tech.

As a born-again Christian, Derick's faith is integral to his life. He is an active member of the North Central Assemblies of God Church in Spring, Texas, where he finds strength and inspiration through fellowship with other believers. Derick strongly believes in God, family, and Christian family values, which are central themes in his writing.

Derick has written extensively on various subjects such as business, leadership, personal development, and Christian spirituality. His works are highly regarded for their clarity, insight, and practicality, making them valuable resources for readers from all backgrounds.

Derick Chibilu's commitment to excellence is evident in everything he does. He is a dedicated professional who takes pride in his work and is constantly seeking new ways to improve himself and his craft. Whether he is writing a new book, delivering a speech, or leading a team, Derick brings passion and enthusiasm to every endeavor.

In summary, Derick Chibilu is an inspiring author and business professional who is making a positive impact on the world. His faith, his family, and his commitment to Christian values deeply influence his life and work. Through his writing, Derick has the power to inspire and uplift readers worldwide.

BOOKS BY MR. DERICK CHIBILU

> **Whimsical Wonders:** 50 Tales of Fictional Fun

> **Love As God Intended It:** Faith, Hope, and Love, But the greatest of these is love.

> **The Bible Storybook**: 50 Exciting Stories for Kids (Volume 1)

> **The Bible Storybook:** 46 Parables: Tales of God's Kingdom and Our Lives (Volume 2)

> **The Bible Storybook:** Exploring The Transformative Power of Faith and The Miraculous Acts of Christ (Volume 3)

> **Shadows of Deception** ~The Hidden Secrets~

> **The Basilica Heist:** Shadows Unveiled

> **Vanishing Chains:** As the intricate plot continues to unfold,

> **Whispers of the Silent Shadows"** Part one

> **Beyond the Veil of Celestial Whispers:** Part Two: The Saga Continues

> **The Prophet Elisha's Unseen Paths**

> **Divine Dwelling:** Unveiling the Mysteries of the Tabernacle

> **Divine Dialogue:** Unveiling the Power of A.C.T.S in the Lord's

Author Contact Information

For information and inquiries or to see other books by the author:
Email: *Thecblogger4@gmail.com*
Or
Visit Our Website at:
www.booksbyderickchibilu.com[1]

---

1. *http://www.booksbyderickchibilu.com*

EMBRACING RESILIENCE
EMBRACING
RESILIENCE
A Story of Love Beyond Illness
BY
DERICK CHIBILU
&
ROBERT CHIBILU

Did you love *Embracing Resilience" A Story of Love Beyond Illness*? Then you should read *Whispers of Dawn" Journey of Healing and Rediscovery* by DERICK CHIBILU!

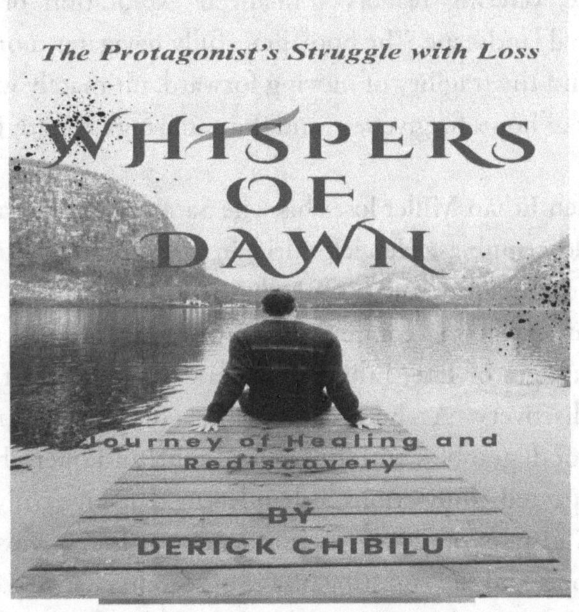

"Whispers of Dawn" is a heartfelt narrative that explores the journey of Ethan Miller through the intricate layers of grief, faith, and the healing power of love. The book captures the essence of the human experience, portraying the protagonist's struggle with loss, the weight of silence, and the solace found in prayer.

Throughout the chapters, the narrative delves into the themes of community support, unexpected connections, and the resilience required for single parenthood. The titles of the chapters, such as "Anchored in Prayer," "A Community of

Comfort," and "A Hand to Hold," reflect the emotional and spiritual aspects of Ethan's voyage toward healing.

The symbolism within the chapter titles, like "The Language of Flowers" and "Footprints in the Sand," adds depth to the narrative, offering readers a nuanced exploration of Ethan's emotional landscape. The book gracefully navigates moments of doubt and the fragility of moving forward, ultimately weaving a tapestry of hope, forgiveness, and the enduring strength found in love.

When Ethan Miller loses his wife Sarah in a tragic accident, his world crumbles. He's left adrift in a sea of grief, clinging to shattered memories and a faith that feels distant. But through the kindness of his community, unwavering prayers, and the gentle nudges of fate, Ethan embarks on a journey of healing and rediscovery. As he navigates the complexities of single parenthood, grapples with lingering doubt, and opens his heart to unexpected connections, Ethan learns that love truly has no end. "Whispers of Dawn" is a poignant tapestry woven with faith, hope, and the enduring power of second chances.

Read more at https://www.booksbyderickchibilu.com/.

About the Author

Derick Chibilu is an upcoming talented author and business professional based in Houston, Texas, where he resides with his beloved wife, Alice, and is known for his inspiring works. Derick holds an MBA from Capella University, a Bachelor of Business in Computer Information Systems from the University of Houston Downtown (UHD), and an Associate of Science in Business Administration from Delaware Tech.

As a born-again Christian, Derick's faith is an integral part of his life. He is an active member of the North Central Assemblies of God Church in Spring, Texas, where he finds strength and inspiration through fellowship with other believers. Derick strongly believes in God, family, and Christian family values, which are central themes in his writing.

Read more at https://www.booksbyderickchibilu.com/.

9 798869 344397